CHAPTER 1

Eric Wizzard, the wizard's boy, hurried home from school. He ran up the path to his front door and stood on tiptoe to reach the big door-knocker.

3

The knocker had a funny face on it.
Eric gave it a good bang.

'Ouch!' said the knocker.

The knocker always said that – ever
since Eric's dad had put a spell on it
by mistake.

'Was there any post today?'
Eric asked the knocker.

Eric's mum was an airline pilot.
She flew all over the world and she
always sent Eric a postcard.

The knocker went into a huff.
Eric was about to bang it again
when the door opened.

Mr Wizzard stood there smiling.
He had a lump of dough in one hand
and a lump of snow in the other.

Eric followed his dad down the hall
to the kitchen.

In the kitchen there were lumps of
dough and lumps of snow everywhere.
And the snow was melting.

Mr Wizzard scooped up all the snow
and placed it in a bowl.

Eric couldn't help feeling worried.
He wished his dad would make meals
the ordinary way.

Eric sighed and bent down to pat the dog.

'What's happened to the dog?' Eric gasped.
Mr Wizzard looked a little embarrassed.

Eric went to the back door and looked
out of the window. Theodore, the real
dog, was on the doorstep and he
looked very unhappy.

CHAPTER 2

Eric's dad began to explain.

15

Eric's dad was a hopeless wizard.
Eric always had to sort out the problems
when his spells went wrong.
'Don't worry, Dad,' said Eric.
'I'll take Tiger to the vet.'
'Good idea,' said Mr Wizzard.
'And I'll have the pizza ready when
you come back.'

Eric hurried out of the house.
He still hadn't had time to read his
mum's postcard.

CHAPTER 3

Eric sat in the vet's waiting room
feeling very uncomfortable.
As Tiger the dog was really
Tiger the cat, he didn't like being
near other dogs.

First of all he
jumped on to
Eric's lap.

Then he tried to get on to Eric's shoulders.

At last it was Eric's turn to see the vet.

'What's he called?' asked the vet.
'He's called Tiger,' said Eric.
'He's got a sore paw.'

The vet lifted Tiger on to the table.
'How did he hurt his paw?' she asked.

The vet looked at Tiger's paw.

The vet gave Tiger a jab to make him feel better.

The vet put a bandage on Tiger's sore paw.

Eric hurried out of the vet's and headed for home. He was getting hungry.

He hoped his dad had the pizza ready.

CHAPTER 4

Eric walked up the path to the front door and gave the knocker a good bang.

BANG - DIDDY - BANG - BANG!
BANG - BANG!

OW! Do you want to knock my teeth out?

LETTERS

Have you read that postcard from your mum yet?

LETTERS

Mind your own business.

Eric was about to tell the knocker what a bossy boots it was, when the door opened.

Eric followed his dad into the kitchen.
It was in a terrible mess.

Eric's mouth began to water. He was
hungry enough to eat a whole pizza.
But the pizza was nowhere to be seen.

'Where is it?' asked Eric.

'Ah!' said his dad. 'I had a little problem with the ham.'

31

Eric went to the back door and looked outside. A tiny hamster was sitting on the doorstep.

'Oh Dad,' said Eric.

'What have you done now?'

Eric's dad began to explain.

The Wizzards now had a cat which looked like a dog and a dog which looked like a hamster. And the little hamster was full of pizza.

'I'll make some scrambled eggs,' said Dad.

CHAPTER 5

Eric waited at the vet's. Theodore was acting very strangely. Although he looked like a hamster he was behaving like a dog. The other people in the waiting room couldn't stop staring.

The vet stared at Eric too.

Eric put Theodore down on the table.

Eric explained about Theodore eating a whole pizza.

The vet gave Theodore some medicine.

The vet gave Eric a funny look.

Eric took Theodore home. He hoped his dad had the scrambled eggs ready. He was really starving.

CHAPTER 6

'Supper in five minutes,' said Dad.
'I must finish cleaning up first.'
'At last,' said Eric. 'I can read Mum's postcard while I'm waiting.'

On the front there was a picture of Hawaii.

On the back she had written...

Dear Eric,
Here's another card to add to your collection.
I hope you're both behaving yourselves!
Love Mum

Eric Wizzard
7 Woody Road
Invertyne
XY50 AB2

At that very moment Mrs Wizzard got out of a taxi.

She walked up the path to the front door.

Mrs Wizzard gave the knocker a
really hard bang.

RAT-TAT-A-TAT-TAT!
TAT-TAT!

Mrs Wizzard usually arrived home at the same time as her postcards.

Eric ran downstairs to open the door.
He hoped his mum wouldn't notice
anything unusual.

His dad had brushed
herbs off the floor.

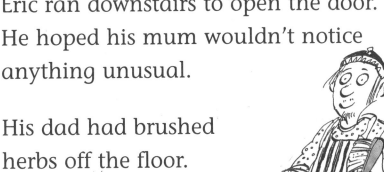

He had wiped cheese
off the doors.

He had scraped
tomato off
the ceiling.

The kitchen looked quite clean after the pizza-making.

Tiger was in his favourite place on top of the wardrobe. He looked like a cat again, although he was still the size of a dog.

Theodore the dog was out in the garden. He was dog-shaped again, although he looked like a pizza.

Eric felt it was safe enough to open the door.

Mum had bought a T-shirt for Eric and a shirt for Dad.

She had also brought dinner.

The Wizzards sat down to eat. The pizza was delicious but Eric's mum wasn't so sure.

'There's not enough tomato on this pizza,' she said. 'I could do with a dash of tomato sauce.'
Eric saw a twinkle in his dad's eye.

He held his breath. Suddenly the sauce
bottle floated out of the cupboard...

...and came down gently on the table.

Dad winked at Eric. Sometimes, just
sometimes, the magic worked.